# A Home for

# Hana

# A Home for

# Hana

Written and Illustrated by

Karen Seymour

ISBN: 9781731056238

To Skyler and Brooke, thanks for the inspiration

High on the mountainside, between the forest and the mountain's rocky crown, is a belt of vivid green that bursts into a colorful riot of wildflowers during its brief summer. Lured by the meadow's richness, mountain goats descend from their lofty, rocky rooks to feed.

One afternoon, a little goat named Hana romped happily through the flowers while her mother browsed nearby. As much as Hana reveled in the meadow's lushness, she dreaded the steep cliffs that loomed just beyond. Being high up, surrounded by loose rocks and sheer walls terrified Hana. So when her mother announced that it was time to go, Hana protested as usual, "But I don't want to go up! It's too scary!"

Mama Goat understood her little one's fear, and patiently answered as she had many times before, "Hana, you know that the steep cliffs protect us from predators. Our hooves can grip the rocks tightly, so we are very agile in rugged places. Our camouflage helps us vanish into our surroundings. Our strong leaps carry us all over the mountainside. And, from high up, we can see any danger approaching for miles."

Although Hana continued to plead, Mama Goat headed resolutely toward the towering rocks and skillfully began scaling the rock face. Hana knew she had to follow. After scrambling to a low ledge, she turned to face a much higher outcropping that she would have to leap to. But the half-hearted hop she gave was not strong enough, and Hana felt herself slip. As her flailing hooves lost contact with the rock, she fell down amid a cascade of pebbles. From high above, Mama Goat heard the commotion and began to hurry back down.

Shaking herself free of the rubble, Hana had only one thought: she could never climb those rocks again! Without pausing, she turned and ran swiftly through the meadow and into increasingly dense stands of trees, until she finally slowed down among strange new surroundings. Instead of endless blue sky stretching overhead, a canopy of trees blocked out the light. Instead of a sea of grass and flowers, underbrush grew thickly.

For a moment, Hana considered turning back. However, her swiveling ears caught the sound of a watery trickle up ahead, and thirst from her mad dash pulled her toward a clear, icy stream. After drinking deeply, she sank to her knees into an exhausted sleep.

Hana had not been asleep long when a splashing sound awakened her. She looked up to see three whiskery faces peering curiously at her from within the swirling stream. Thinking of the golden marmots of the meadow, Hana asked in confusion, "What are you doing in the water? I thought marmots lived on the meadow!"

Three laughs came as a reply. "The what live on the where?" giggled one of the smaller animals.

Smiling, the largest one explained, "We're otters, not marmots. We live in streams and rivers, not the meadow."

Hana had never considered that animals might live in the water. Then a thought began to form: if otters could make their home in a stream, maybe she could too. Then she would never have to ascend a mountainside again!

"The water is your home?" she asked.

"It's where we find food and escape our predators," answered the mother otter.

"And play!" added one of the pups, pouncing on his sister.

"Otters are great at swimming," explained the sister pup as she and her brother wrestled and rolled.

It sounded just right to Hana, except she wasn't sure whether goats could swim. But the streambed, she noticed, was made of rocks. Didn't Mama Goat often tell her how great goat hooves were for navigating rocks?

All uncertainty gone, Hana declared, "I want to live in the water too! Can I join you?"

The mother otter looked surprised, but the pups shouted gleefully, "Yes! Join us!"

Hana jumped with a tremendous SPLASH into the stream. The delighted pups cavorted in the waves, but Hana gasped in shock. The water was freezing! She didn't realize that, while the otters' dense fur kept them comfortable in the icy water, a goat's white fluff offered no such protection.

Struggling against the current, hooves slipping wildly over the slick streambed, Hana thrashed and splashed helplessly until she finally managed to clamber out of the stream, shivering and soaked.

"Do it again!" cheered the pups. Mama Otter shook her head and dove under the water. With friendly waves of their paws, the pups followed her downstream.

"That didn't work," Hana muttered, shaking out her soggy coat and turning away from the stream to head uphill through the forest. "But surely I can find a different kind of home."

After traveling for a while, Hana suddenly stopped short.  She hadn't realized that she had been passing by an animal until the large-eyed, large-eared head of a fawn turned and their curious gazes met.

"I thought deer lived on the meadow," Hana said in surprise.

Glancing around cautiously, the fawn whispered, "We graze in the meadow, but the forest is really much safer."

"It's safer?" asked Hana interestedly.  She thought she might have an easier time living down among the trees than high among the rocks.  "But aren't there predators in the forest?"

The fawn answered quietly, "Yes.  That's why my mother hides me here.  If I lie very still, they pass right by without seeing me, like you almost did.  It's because I have such great camouflage," he added proudly.

Excitement mounted as Hana pondered.  The fawn used his camouflage to hide from predators.  Didn't Mama Goat often remind her how great a goat's camouflage was?

"Then I am going to hide in the forest using *my* camouflage," she decided.

"Shhhh," warned the fawn.  "You need to find some brush to hide under. And be quiet!"

Nodding silently, Hana tiptoed to what looked like the perfect spot and lay still. The best part about her new home was the parade of animals who came to investigate her. After a while, though, she began to suspect that something wasn't right. A glance at the fawn revealed that he was not hosting even a single visitor. Overhead in the branches, some squirrels began making a game of showering her with leaves. "This will help you hide!" one of them snickered.

Positive now that something had gone wrong, Hana sadly rose as the squirrels began aiming pinecones at her. Glancing back, she saw that the fawn had not stirred except to follow her departure with his huge, somber eyes.

Hana resumed her uphill trek through the woods. Gradually the trees became smaller, and the gaps between them were filled with grass and sunlight. Hana's attention was drawn by movement in a nearby tree.

Hopping from branch to branch, a pair of finches twittered cheerily while pecking at insects. Hana called out to them, "Excuse me!"

Startled, the finches stopped fluttering and looked down.

"I was wondering," Hana began, "do you two actually live in a tree?"

"Of course we do," one finch chirped in surprise. "Where else would we live? On the ground?" Both birds twittered with amusement as they resumed their activity.

"But why not live on the ground?" Hana persisted. "I do."

Again the finches stopped, and one peeped down in a horrified voice, "But it's not safe down there!"

"You'd be much safer in a tree," the second finch advised. Then, forgetting all about Hana, the two birds happily returned to their hopping and pecking.

Hana surveyed the tree doubtfully. It didn't look like a home to her at all, but the finches had assured her that it was. But how could she get into a tree? She couldn't fly up like the birds could—but didn't her mother often mention how great mountain goats are at jumping?

Ready to test her idea, Hana leaped at the branches. The finches' happy chirps became screeches when Hana crashed down on a branch, which cracked loudly as it sent the poor goat tumbling to the ground. She untangled herself and looked up sheepishly to find that the tree was empty. The birds had flitted off to find a more peaceful tree.

Disappointed, Hana trudged onward to the meadow. Her spirits lifted at the sight of her favorite place. She wandered and grazed, absorbed in soft breezes and sweet smells. A little blue butterfly landed on a nearby flower and spread delicate wings to catch the waning afternoon sunlight.

Immediately Hana asked, "Do you live in a flower?"

"Flowers are my food," corrected the tiny voice. "All the meadow's my home."

Hana gasped. "The whole meadow's your home? But it isn't safe, is it?"

"Of course it is," replied the butterfly, wings beating slowly. "It provides me with everything I need." With that, the insect took flight, a miniature cerulean sky-flake floating above the flowers.

"I knew it," cried Hana, "It *is* safe here!  The meadow will be my home now!  If I can find Mama, I can tell her…!"

Eagerly Hana began running and calling for her mother.  But when she paused to listen for a reply, something made her suddenly stiffen, heart pounding.  The light breeze, which had been delivering messages of fresh grass and abundant blooms, was suddenly tinged with something dangerous.

For the first time, Hana felt hemmed in by the meadow.   Her view was limited, and the trees that dotted the grass seemed to hide secrets in their shadows.  Remembering her mother's advice that goats needed high places to have good views, Hana trotted nervously to a large boulder and climbed up.

Hana tested the breeze for another hint of the threatening smell. There! Her keen eyes focused on a small stand of trees. Weaving sinuously between them like a silent, tawny wave stalked a cougar.

Although a terrible threat here on the ground, a cougar was usually no match for a sure-footed goat among the rocks. For the first time, those steep rocks seemed like a sanctuary to Hana. Could she reach them in time? She would have to try. Had the cougar seen her yet?

Even as the question formed, her terrified brown eyes locked with the steady amber ones below. Both creatures froze. With a frightened cry, Hana whirled around, and lunged frantically toward the welcoming heights just ahead. As soon as Hana moved, the cougar also leaped into motion, swallowing up huge swaths of ground with each powerful stride.

Aware that the predator was swiftly closing the gap between them, Hana cried out again. From overhead came the answering bleat of her mother, who had spent the afternoon searching for a sign of Hana. Now, she saw the danger and was hurtling down the mountainside like a wooly white torpedo.

Hana charged at the rocks, launching herself toward the lowest ledge. She felt rather than saw the cougar gliding through the air behind her, paws outstretched and claws unsheathed. His shadow engulfed her as he closed the last of the distance between them.

Just as Hana's hooves grabbed the rock shelf, she felt the brush of a heavy paw—and then it fell aside. Sharp horns lowered, Mama Goat had leaped at the cat and sent him crashing to the ground. Snarling furiously, he swiped at her, but she was already racing up the mountainside.

Meanwhile, Hana had taken advantage of the precious seconds her mother had given her and was rapidly surging upward. She finally emerged from her climb atop a snow-covered crag. Panting, she looked around. She had lost her mother yet again, and below her was the cougar, determinedly clawing along the steep rock. He paused to scan the rocks above him. Hana breathed in sharply as his gaze swept over her—and then past her. He hadn't seen her! He searched patiently for many long moments, motionless except for a tiny twitch at the tip of his tail.

Standing as frozen as the snow that now concealed her, Hana watched as the cougar at last turned to descend, disappearing ghostlike into the shadows far below. Then she looked up to see, as if from a dream, Mama Goat crossing the snow toward her.

Dashing up to her mother, Hana had never felt happier or more relieved. She now understood that she had had everything she needed all along. Her hooves, so useless on the slippery stones of the stream, were nimble and unwavering up here. Her white coat, which had attracted every eye in the forest, concealed her against the mountain's snow. Her powerful muscles, which would never help her into a tree, had allowed her to ascend where her enemy could not. And her far-seeing eyes told her that danger had passed. As she and her mother turned to join their herd, Hana knew that this was the home where she belonged.

# Facts About Hana's Home

Mighty **Mt.Rainier** towers over the Washington landscape, rising up to 14,411 feet. This active volcano is not only one of the tallest peaks in the US, but also the most glaciated. One of its many glaciers is the **Ohanapecosh,** whose name means "standing at the edge." Hana the mountain goat takes her name from this glacier.

Gracing the shoulders of Mt. Rainier between elevations of about 4,500 to 6,500 feet, the glorious **Subalpine Meadows** explode into bloom during an approximately 45-day growing season. Snow lingers here even in the summer, and trees grow sparsely, disappearing altogether above 6,500 feet.

**Mountain Goats** are not true goats, but related to both goats and antelopes. Predation of mountain goat is relatively rare due to their mastery of a rocky habitat that most predators find inaccessible. Slipping and falling is actually a greater danger to goats, especially young ones. Their wide-spreading, rough-padded cloven hooves enable them to be excellent climbers. They are also great jumpers, able to make leaps up to 12 feet long.

Capable of holding their breath for up to 4 minutes, **River Otters** are well suited to semiaquatic life. Their thick coats trap air bubbles which help insulate them, and the under layer of fur is exceptionally dense. This is how they are able to stay comfortable even in frigid water. They are very playful, and have been seen making games of sliding off rocks into the water, and even dropping pebbles into the water and catching them on their foreheads!

Emerging with the nascent spring foliage, the **Columbia Black-Tailed Deer** fawn is tucked away by its mother in a hiding spot while she goes to feed. Its spotted saddle, hiding behavior, and lack of scent for the first few days of life all help keep it safe from predators. Blacktail deer range from Northern California to Alaska, and can frequently be found at the edges of forests.

**Gray-Crowned Rosy Finches** inhabit mountain ranges throughout the Northwest down to California, and some islands such as the Aleutians. Flocks of these finches can be found foraging for seeds and insects in trees and on the ground.

The **Anna Blue Butterfly** is a species of tiny butterfly found in Northwestern mountains above an elevation of 3,000 feet, typically from June to August.

With a larger range than any other land mammal in the Western Hemisphere, the **Cougar** can be found anywhere from the Yukon to the Andes. This big stalking cat hunts animals as large as deer, elk, and moose, to as small as rabbits, rodents, and insects.

Made in the USA
San Bernardino, CA
18 December 2019